KAY THOMPSON'S *ELOISE*

Eloise Has a Lesson

STORY BY **Margaret McNamara**
ILLUSTRATED BY **Kathryn Mitter**

READY-TO-READ

SIMON SPOTLIGHT
NEW YORK   LONDON   TORONTO   SYDNEY

ABDO
Spotlight

ABDOPUBLISHING.COM

Reinforced library bound edition published in 2016 by Spotlight,
a division of ABDO, PO Box 398166, Minneapolis, Minnesota 55439.
Spotlight produces high-quality reinforced library bound editions for
schools and libraries. Published by agreement with Simon Spotlight.

Printed in the United States of America, North Mankato, Minnesota.
042015
092015

THIS BOOK CONTAINS
RECYCLED MATERIALS

SIMON SPOTLIGHT
An imprint of Simon & Schuster Children's Publishing Division
1230 Avenue of the Americas, New York, NY 10020
Copyright © 2005 by the Estate of Kay Thompson

LIBRARY OF CONGRESS CATALOGING-IN-PUBLICATION DATA

This title was previously cataloged with the following information:

McNamara, Margaret.
Eloise has a lesson / written by Margaret McNamara ;
illustrated by Kathryn Mitter.— 1st ed.
p. cm. — (Ready-to-read) (Kay Thompson's Eloise)
Summary: Eloise would rather tease her tutor,
Philip, than let him teach her math.
ISBN 0-689-87367-0 (pbk.)
[1. Teachers—Fiction. 2. Teasing—Fiction. 3. Arithmetic—Fiction.]
I. Mitter, Kathy, ill. II. Title. III. Series. IV. Series: Kay Thompson's Eloise.
PZ7.M47879343En 2005
[E]—dc22
2004009343

978-1-61479-405-9 (reinforced library bound edition)

Spotlight
A Division of ABDO
abdopublishing.com

I am Eloise.
I am six.

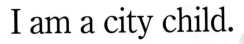

I am a city child.

I live in a hotel
on the tippy-top floor.

This is Philip.

He is my tutor.
He is no fun.

Here is what I do not like:
doing math
for one half hour
in the morning.

Here is what I like:
teasing Philip.

Philip says, "Hello, Eloise."

I say, "Hello, Eloise."

Philip says, "Math time."

I say, "Bath time?"

Philip says, "Eloise, please."

I say, "Eloise, please."

Philip says,
"What is five plus six?"

I say, "You do not know?"

"Nanny!" says Philip.
"Make Eloise behave."
"Eloise, behave," says Nanny.

Chalk makes a very good straw.

"What is five plus six?"
says Philip.

"Five plus six is the same as
six plus five," I say.

Philip says, "Oh, Eloise."

I say, "Oh, Eloise."

Nanny says,
"Math time is nearly over.

"Time to finish up, up, up."

Philip says, "Eloise."

I say, "Philip."

Philip says, "Think."

I say, "I am thinking."

Philip says,
"What is five plus six?"

"It is eleven," I say.
"And the lesson is over."

Ooooooooo,
I absolutely love math.